THE
NUTCRACKER RETURNS

KA EVANS

ARPress
ILLUMINATING IDEAS.
EMPOWERING VOICES

ARPress
45 Dan Road Suite 36
Canton MA 02021

Hotline: 1(800) 220-7660
Fax: 1(855) 752-6001

Ordering Information:
Quantity Sales. Special discounts are available on quantity purchases by corporations, associations, and others. For details, contact the publisher at the address above.

Printed in the United States of America.

ISBN-13   Paperback   979-8-89389-823-1
                        eBook   979-8-89389-824-8

Library of Congress Control Number: 2024923233

It is 1878 in Britain, the sky was a thick grey and the wind whispering through the trees while the famous De La Tour house stood silent in grieve. For the news had spread that Nathan De La Tour had died leaving behind his grieving widow and children.

Snow was falling heavily from above while the blowing wind whipped in every direction and in the large field behind the house stood the beautiful Clara Marie De La Tour, the only daughter of the late master.

Her long brown hair tied in ribbons, her cheeks were pink as well as her small nose, from the cold wind and her light blue eyes were filled with tears. She wore a long black dress and a matching bonnet with a black coat down to her feet; her sleeves reached her upper arms and her neckline was frilly just above her chest. If you looked into her eyes you could see sadness, for she and her 12 year old brother Timmy were leaving their home with their mother.

Clara looked around her back garden with its many flowers and beyond the fields, wishing there was a way she could stay. "Clara" Clara sighed as she recognised her mother's voice, "It's time we were off" her mother called,

Clara shook her head and began to walk slowly to the front of the house where she met her mother who wore a light purple gown with black frilly sleeves and her blond hair in a bun with sad green eyes and Timmy wore grey breaches, a white vest, black polished shoes, a long black and silver coat and a small hat, he had a head of wiled red hair and hazel eyes. Clara's mother Ella smiled softly to her.

"It is Christmas eve, why can't we stay here for Christmas?" Clara asked her.

But Ella shook her head "We can't Clara, your grandparents are waiting and everyone is ready to meet their new Prince and Princess of their country" she said sadly as she had also wanted to stay.

Timmy quickly grabbed his umbrella before he locked the door behind him then turned to his mother "Why didn't dad tell us he was a prince?" he asked in confusion, usally their father told them everything, even if it was about busness.

Ella smiled with a faraway look on her face as if she was remembering something pleasant "Because we wanted our children to have a normal life but now that your father and your uncle are gone there is no one else to take the throne except for you two" they stood quietly listening to the peaceful air until a noise broke the silence.

They turned towards the pathway to see a large black carriage with golden wheels, four white horses pulling it along through the grey old gates to settle before them and a group of royal guards on black horses surrounded the carriage.

The lead man got down from his horse, walked to open the carriage door and bowed "I am honoured to welcome you Princess Ella, Princess Clara and Prince Timmy, let me introduce myself, I am Stanley Cross the first royal guard" Ella and Clara curtsied while Timmy bowed back before they climbed silently into the carriage.

"Thank you for picking us up Mr Cross" Ella said as Stanley smiled warmly, nodded his head than jumped back onto his horse.

They travelled for hours, each deciding what to do with their rooms but Timmy was more exited on getting food, Clara shook her head at her little brother over her book that she always carry with her "Honestly Timmy, we had breakfast like two hours ago….I think" Clara said a little annoyed and amused.

Across from her Timmy began to sulk and rubbing his belly "But I can't help it Clara I am a growing boy and growing boys need food" he whined, Clara signed and gave him her apple while in the corner of the carriage Ella laughed at her children behaviour.

When they finally pulled to a stop Timmy glanced through the blinds then looked back with wide eyes and a pale face. Clara frowned at his horror struck expression "What is it Timmy?" she asked worriedly while their mother stared.

Timmy swallowed loudly and said "There's a crowd out there and we are in front of a pink palace" before Clara could answer the carriage door was pulled open and Stanley Cross held out a hand to help the ladies climb down. As soon as they were out the carriage was pulled away and the crowd erupted into a loud happy cheer, some was throwing flowers, others was singing a song while the rest was clapping and smiling at them.

Ella walked up ahead while Clara stayed behind with Tommy holding his hand for she knew he didn't like crowds of people staring at him. they walked along a red and green carpet that lead to the castle doors and standing in front of them was the king and queen.

Both the King and Queen was wearing golden clothes and crowns. The king had red hair and hazel eyes, he was tall with broad shoulders while the queen was the older copy of Clara, she was almost as tall as her husband. Everyone fell silent when they reached the royal couple because it was no secret that the King and Queen had disapproved of her son's choice for a bride.

They stared at each other for a minute then the queen gave a big smile and stepped forward. She took Ella's hands while kissing her on the cheek "Welcome home Ella my dear" she greeted her daughter-in-law warmly.

Ella smiled back "Thank you for having us your majesty" Ella started but was interrupted by the King.

The king stepped beside his wife and placed an arm on Ella's shoulder while saying "None of that, you must call us mom and dad. We are family now like Nathan wanted us to be" Ella nodded as her smile grew bigger.

Clara looked at the palace, it was bright pink and had large windows with one tower. She looked over to see Timmy being welcomed by their grandparents. Clara watched as the King patted Tommy's wiled red hair. He had their father's hair but Timmy had their mother's long cheek bones and small nose but now Clara could see he got his eyes from their grandfather. At that moment Clara's grandparents turned their attentions onto her.

They had a good look at her before the Queen bent forward and kissed her cheek, that's when Clara noticed just how much she resembles the Queen. Clara had their mothers soft lips and her father's eyes but the rest was from her grandmother. The King also kissed her cheek as the Queen spoke "Why, you look just like me when I was your age……except you have your father's eyes" her grandmother said happily.

The king smiled as he looked between them "You are right my love, she does look like you" then he looked to the silent crowd "My people" the king shouted to them "I would like to introduce to you my daughter in law and grandchildren…..Princess Ella De La Tour, Princess Clara Marie De La Tour and Prince Timmy John De La Tour" the people cheered again as the royal family walked together through the large doors and into the palace.

In another world stood a very dark kingdom where the sky's was always deep grey like storm clouds that never pour, where people lived in fear and where a vicious ruler called the Mouse King lived.

He was a very mean King to his subjects and he was half mouse and half man. His hair was long and black, his ears round, pointed and a bit larger than normal ears, his eyes a dark shade of red and he had a long tale.

The Mouse King stood by the library window, gazing out at the darken lands when a knock came at the door, he looked around to see his Mouse Guards standing there "What is it?" he demanded.

The Guard cowered under the Mouse Kings dark eyes "I am sorry sire but he has escaped" the guard whimpered.

The Mouse King hissed as he grabbed the mouse by his shirt "Do you realised what you have done, he will try to take the kingdom back" the guards cowered further away from him as he let go of the shirt and pointed at the door "Get every good guard and get him back"

"But sire" the guard complained "We don't know where he is"

The Mouse King paused then looked at his guards with a cruel smile "Get me something that belongs to the Prince" the guards rushed out as the Mouse King sat at his desk with the smile still in place "He can't defeat me this time" he whispered to himself "Years ago he had help from his friends, his people and that girl but this time, he has no one" he looked down at the jewel necklace that he wore "With this necklace I can have anything I want" at that moment the guards ran back in and held out a hair brush. the Mouse King pulled out a piece of the Prince's hair and held it up high while the other hand was over the necklace and he said.

"*Magic of the Christmas Angel Dee,*
I call on you to help me,
Track him down where ever he go,
With this hair his essence shall flow"

The necklace glowed until the hair changed into a shiny blue stone.

The Mouse King smiled and gave the stone to the guard "Take this, it will show you where to find him. now go" the guards bowed then left just as he started to laugh.

Clara looked around her new room as she was putting her things away. Her walls was purple, she had a large window that had a view of the gardens, a king-sized bed by another door that leads to her bathroom, a cabinet that held her gowns and a makeup table on the other side of the bed.

Clara changed into a light green gown with patterns of leafs. When she was walking down for dinner she saw that her mother and grandparents was talking. Clara was about to knock when she heard her own name and her mother's shocked voice "You want Clara to get married?" Ella asked "She is too young"

The King said "Ella. Clara is 18 years old and it is about time she meets someone" Clara turned around to see Timmy coming towards her so she placed a finger to her lips telling him to stay quiet.

He giggled in his hands when they heard the Queen say "Clara is a beautiful young woman, its time she got married and started a family of her own" the Queen said calmly.

Ella signed "Maybe it is time I let her go but I want Clara to choose her own husband. No one else will choose for her" she stated while the king and queen agreed.

Finally Clara knocked the door lightly of the dining room and they entered. After dinner they sat in the sitting room looking at the tree and listening to Timmy talk of tomorrow when suddenly he frowned as he saw a sad look cross Clara's face "What's the matter Clara?" he asked in confusion as he knew Clara loved Christmas and for the last view years she had been unhappy.

Everyone turned to look at her so she shrugged "It will be the first Christmas without father" she explained in a small voice.

Ella smoothed the hair from her face "I know sweetie but your father would not want you to be unhappy on Christmas" Clara nodded but she was also sad because of a Prince many years ago that got his way into her heart. The prince she's craving to love but the Prince she knew she would never see again. It almost brought tears to her eyes at the thought of him, Clara shook her head to clear and listened to the conversation again.

The Queen smiled "I remember when Nathan was a small bo. He would silently go down stairs to the Christmas tree and would see if he can sneak a present without us knowing" everyone laughed.

Then the King said "I remember one Christmas when he had a train set, he danced around the room in happiness" he informed his grandchildren.

It was hours later when the clock chimed 11 o'clock. Ella stood up and said "Ok. time for bed" Clara and Timmy said good night and went up to their rooms.

In an old abandoned factory where the Prince rested. He looked at his wooden hand with sad eyes. The spell that the Mouse King had put on him had turned him into a Nutcracker once again, then they locked him up into the darkest tower but he had escaped only by luck and borrowed magic "Christmas Angel" he called "If you can hear me. please help me" a vision of a tall woman appeared before him.

She wore a long silver dress, shoulder length sunny blond hair with tinsels and ribbons in it and large golden wings out stretched from her back, "Christmas Angel" he began "I don't know what to do. The Mouse King is back. he took my Kingdom and turned me back into a Nutcracker but he is stronger this time" he said urgently.

The Christmas Angel signed sadly "There is nothing I can do Prince Daniel, the Mouse King have stolen my powerful necklace so I can't help.......but there is someone who can" the Prince looked up at her, his face full of hope.

"Who?" he begged.

The Christmas Angel smiled "You know her in your head as well as your heart. Think back for when this first happened" she said.

Prince Daniel closed his eyes as pain crashed through his chest and when he whispered that one name, it was filled with deep love and an endless sorrow "Clara"

The Christmas Angel nodded "Yes she can help us again….hold out your hand" he did what the Angel instructed then the Christmas Angel dropped something into the Princes palm. He looked down to see a necklace with a red heart with white wings and looked back up at the Christmas Angel who smiled "It is a gift for Clara. There are five wishes' in this necklace for her. She could use them on your quest" the Christmas Angel informed.

Prince Daniel smiled "Thank you Christmas Angel" he said as he ran towards the doors.

Before he left the Christmas Angel called out after him "But Prince Daniel don't stay there for too long, I think the Mouse King put a tracking spell on you. Please be careful" he nodded, waved and ran out.

Prince Daniel ran to the portals between worlds and turned it on to find Clara, a wall of yellow light appeared, rising from the ground. With a deep breath Prince Daniel stepped into the shimmering light and came out into a large pink palace "She must be here" he whispered as he crept through the halls.

• • •

Clara was lying on her side in bed facing the window, watching little bits of snow fall. She was almost asleep when she felt her quilt being pulled lightly and heard a familiar voice call to her "Clara?" Clara slowly opened her eyes convinced she was dreaming of her lost love. She looked around then the whisper came again "Clara. turn around" Clara sat up strait and looked to the other side of the bed. There she saw a shape and in thinking it was a rat, Clara grabbed a pillow from behind her and tried hitting it until he spoke again "Clara stop, it is me Daniel" she paused the pillow in mid-air then slowly lowered the pillow and took the candle that sat on her nightstand to see the shape.

Clara saw a wooden soldier but older then the last time they had met, though still familiar. The same handsome face, black long hair smoothed back that she wished she could sink her fingers through now that it was wooden, those lips she had once kissed and his glittering brown eyes. "Daniel but I do not understand. We broke the spell years ago, why are you a nutcracker again?" she asked in confusion.

"I don't have much time, please get dress and meet me near the Christmas tree" before she could answer Prince Daniel jumped down from the bed and walked out of the room.

When Clara was ready, she walked down to the sitting room where the tree was. She wore a long pink and red gown with a high neckline and long sleeves that covered her arms and her brown hair was running down her back and over her shoulders. Clara found the Prince under the tree and watching the glowing lights. It made her heart flutter seeing the joy on his face.

Prince Daniel turned around when he heard her footsteps, his expression softened as he looked at her and met her eyes. For years he had been dreaming of Clara. Wishing every moment that he could somehow be with her, make her his wife, raise their children and even hold her every night to their dying day "You are more beautiful than even I imagined" he said softly.

Clara blushed and gave him a shy smile "Thank you Prince Daniel" she said politely.

The Prince sighed "You might as well call me nutcracker while I am in this form….I need your help again Clara. The Mouse King has returned and more powerful because of a necklace he stole from the Christmas Angel. She can't help me because without that necklace her powers are cut in half and the only way to break the spell is to get the necklace back from the Mouse King or to destroy it" Prince Daniel explained.

Clara listened carefully then shook her head "I will still call you Daniel but I thought we got rid of him the last time"

Daniel shrugged "So did I" he stated sadly.

Clara sat into a chair, looking out at the snowy night as flakes started covering everything then turned back to the Prince "I would if I could but I am too big to go through the portal again" she said tearfully as she really wanted to help her love.

Daniel walked over until he was standing near her legs and looked up at her "I have something that could help" he replied then he held out the necklace to her.

"Oh" Clara gasped at the beautiful piece "It is beautiful Daniel"

When Clara's fingers touched the necklace, the chain grew big so it could fit Clara`s neck "Now" the Prince said when she put in on "Say I wish to be small" he instructed her.

Clara stared at him until he nodded "Ok…I wish I could be small" the heart began to glow a bright white light that surrounded her body. Clara stood up when she realised that her figure was shrinking. Just when she was under eye level with Daniel did it stop.

Clara looked around the now large sitting room, everything was bigger than her, the chairs was bigger, the table was bigger, the toys was bigger even the Christmas decorations was bigger than she was. Clara glanced over to the Prince "How did that happen? Last time the Ice queen had to shrink me" she asked.

The Prince held up his hands "It was the Christmas Angels magic this time, she asked me to give it to you. It holds five wishes….well four now but she did it for you when you need them" she nodded but was disappointed that it was not from him. Daniel held out his hand to her "It is time to go Clara" Clara took his wooden hand into hers and together they walked carefully into the garden where there was snow covered fountains, on the side there was designs of hearts, stars and swans.

Daniel walked up to a swan and touched its beak. the swans beak turned downwards and slowly the wings folded up to make a hole. Daniel pointed at the hole and said "Portal of this realm open the portal to my kingdom" inside the hole a shining light appeared, Clara looked towards Daniel's who bowed while saying "After you" she smiled and walked into the light.

Clara came out in to a land that looked in ruin when the Prince came out she grabbed his hand "What happened?" she asked in shock.

Daniel signed sadly "When the Mouse King came back, he was angry because we stopped him once before. So after turning me into a nutcracker, he made the buildings old and crumbling, the trees withered and died and the rivers stopped flowing. The people who lived here were sent into the prisons or was turned into animals, statues or in hiding, the skies are endless shadows and unless we can get that necklace way from him, it will stay this way".

Clara stared at the dark kingdom "So" she said "What do we do first?"

Daniel started to walk not towards the kingdom but towards the remaining forest "First" Daniel started "We find the old Captain of my guards, Captain Snow, then we go to the Snow Queen and rescue my guardians from their magic prison" Clara nodded silently. As they walked deeper into the forest they started to hear strange noises behind them. Daniel looked back to see the mouse guards trying to sneak up on them but when they realised they were curt the mouse guards ran after them. Daniel grabbed Clara's hand and forced her to run "Do not stop Clara, they are behind us" Clara took a peek behind her to see the mouse guards that's half men and half mouse in black and yellow uniforms chasing them.

She turned to Daniel "How do they look like that. Last time I saw them they were just over grown mice?" she asked in confusion.

Daniel shook his head while running "The Mouse King cast a spell to turn them human but it went wrong, he did not have the power to do it, so now they are men with tales, elf ears and different colour eyes" just up ahead of them was an old church, two walls was standing up, the door and other walls were crumbling near the ground, there also was a cross still hanging above the doors and on the other side there was a burial ground full of new graves.

Daniel and Clara hide into the abandoned churched where there was a large hole in the ground. They climbed inside and covered the top with the upper table, in the hole Daniel and Clara tensed as they heard the mouse guards moving around the wrecked room "Where are they?" one asked as they moved closer.

"Who was that woman with the Prince?" another asked.

"I don't know but the king will not be happy that he got away" Clara and Daniel signed in relieve when they heard the guards walk away.

• • •

At the castle the Mouse King was livid, storming around the room shouting at his guards "YOU LOST HIM" he yelled angrily, thunder rumbled outside "I give you one order but you could not even do that" the guards cringed at the kings fury as he glared at them.

"I am sorry my lord it was working fine but then this morning the tracker just stopped" a fearful guard explained.

The King shook his head "It should have worked, I never make mistakes" he said as he walked to his desk.

"Sire I think I know why it stopped" the mouse king turned around to see Coro his second in command.

"What is it Coro" the King demanded.

Coro sauntered over to stand by the king's side "When we found the Prince, he was not alone. There was a young lady with him and I believe that her presence has stopped the tracker from finding him"

The Mouse King froze "There is no woman left they are either in my prisons or turned into animals. Unless…….no he could not have found her" he hissed darkly.

Coro waited while staring at the King "Who my lord?" he asked.

The Mouse King looked at the new guards then said "Get out" they both bowed and left the room. When the door was thermally shut he turned to Coro "let me tell you a story, years ago when the Prince was a child I turned him into a nutcracker and took his kingdom" Coro frowned but before he could ask, the king said "Yes I turned him into a nutcracker again" he leaned back into his chair with a smirk on his face "Anyway, it was then that he met a little girl called Clara Marie De La Tour, she came into my kingdom, broke all my spells and took it back but this time, oh no-no this time I have the power, she will not defeat me again" he gave Coro a cruel nasty smilcd "let's go and meet an old friend" the Mouse King chuckled as he strolled to the door.

* * *

Clara and Daniel stopped by a twisted bent tree "Why have we stopped?" Clara asked gently.

Daniel looked around the trees then started to smile before shouting out into the air "Snow, hay Snow, I know you are out there" there was a cracking sound in the bushes then someone jumped out of the trees to land at Daniels feet and there stood was Captain Snow. He was a tall man, white long hair and beard and he was wearing a long red and yellow stared coat with black legging and boots. The Captain and Daniel stared at each other than with a shout they clapped each other on the backs and started laughing.

Clara could not help but smile at the two men, when they finally settled down Captain Snow looked over at Clara then starred in shock "Miss Clara, it's been what 11 years and you have grown into a beauty" he exclaimed.

They smiled as he hugged her "It is good to see you too, Captain Snow" she said cheerfully.

The Captain signed and let her go "Are you here to help us again?" he asked gently, though he wasn't happy about it as they had almost lost her last time.

Clara nodded silently while Daniel said "let's go, we have to get to the Snow Queen" he said as he carefully took Clara's hand.

Clara cleared her throat "How alike are the Snow Queen and the Ice Queen?" she asked hesitantly.

Daniel smiled "Very alike because the Ice Queen is the Snow Queen's mother"

"Oh" she replied as the men nodded and started towards the snowy mountain where the Snow Queen lived, but unknown to them the Mouse King was hidden behind them and when he set his eyes on Clara's lovely face he was determined to have her as his own.

They just got to the edge of the mountain line where the snow started when a voice called from behind them "Well, well, well look what we have here" they whirled around to see the mouse king standing near the forest, a huge smiled glued to his face "My wooden nutcracker" Daniel glared at him "Our captive Captain Snow" the Captain crossed his arms and turned his head away but still keeping watch in the corner of his eye "And" the Mouse King took one step forward, his red glowing eyes fixed on Clara's face "The lovely rose of the group……Miss Clara Marie De La Tour" with every word he spoke he took a step towards her. Daniel and Captain Snow moved to stand in front of Clara, blocking the Mouse Kings path but he just smiled then clicked his fingers that caused his guards to appear out of the trees to stand behind him "You have grown into quit a beautiful lady Miss Clara, we will talk later when we are alone" he pointed at them then shouted "Get them" the guards ran onward at his orders.

Daniel pushed Clara towards the mountain "Hurry, run to the keypoint" he said urgently.

As they began to run Clara asked breathlessly "What is the keypoint?" Daniel took hold of Clara's hand and she almost stopped when she felt a tingling sensation spread through her hand.

"See that pole with a light and that is decorated of hearts, stars and snowflakes" he waited until she nodded to continue "Well, it is the keypoint line between kingdoms. My father and the Snow Queens father became best friends, if one was in trouble they would meet at the keypoint and the other would help" he told her as they ran faster.

Clara raised her eyebrows "I am surprised your fathers did not get you two to marry"

Daniel looked at Clara to see her cheeks turn pink and gave her a little smile "Actually she married my big brother Nick Rowe" Clara starred at him in shock suddenly Clara tripped then falls to the snowy ground but Daniel could never leave her behind so he placed his hands under her shoulders and legs, lifting her into his arms and ran the rest of the way to the line.

Clara stared up at him, even though he was now made of wood she could still see the boy she loved and his shining light. Clara's heart pounded faster whenever she thinks of him in both a great happiness and sadness for she would never believe he would love her the way she loves him and that is the most heartbroken truth to Clara.

Just as they crossed over the line, the Snow Queen herself appeared, her ice light purple hair flowing behind her, she had sparkly blue skin and bright green eyes with a long tight white and lilac dress, she stared down at the mice that was intruding on to her mountain "STOP" her voice vibrated in the wind and across the hills but the mice just kept coming.

Clara who was still in Daniel's arms signed "I wish there was an avalanched" the heart around her neck started to glow before the mountains began to shake, the ground shifted and slowly giant snow balls started rolling down the hills towards the Mouse King and his guards. When the mice realised what was happening they ran the opposite direction but it was too late the snow collided with the mice and they were thrown back into the forest or berried in the snow, everyone watched as the glowing light slowly fade beck into the necklace.

Daniel smiled "Wow that was powerful…that would mean you have 3 wishes left"

The Snow Queen asked "It is from the Christmas Angel, was it not?" the Snow Queen motioned for them to follow her. Clara and Daniel silently nodded "Well then let us go to my home" she smiled at Daniel "Your brother Nick is here" Daniel gently let Clara down so she could walk but kept her hand, they were walking towards a large purple door that appeared in the rocky walls.

Clara asked "Were you married when I came years ago, Snow Queen?"

The Snow queen shook her head "No that was after the Mouse Kings defeat. Nick could not be there to help Daniel….oops I mean nutcracker" she said the name with

a smirk "Because he had to make plans for their parents funeral"

Clara looked at Daniel "I am so sorry" he just shrugged then the Snow Queen waved her hand in the direction of the door.

"Go on in" she said,

The Snow Queen took them through several halls to walk into a large warm room where there was a fire blazing, the walls was a light blue color, big windows, sitting chairs stood around the fireplace and in one of those chairs was Prince Nick Rowe. Prince Nick walked to his brother but stopped and stared "Daniel, you are a nutcracker again?" he asked in shock "And who is this?"

He held out his hand to Clara while Daniel introduced them "This is Clara Marie De La Tour, Clara this is my elder brother Nick"

Clara smiled as she shook his hand "It is nice to meet you Prince Nick" Clara could see the resemblance between the two brothers, they both have black hair, light brown eyes and perfect built but Prince Nick had a lot more muscles then Daniel.

Prince Nick nodded then turned to face his woody brother "So little brother, tell me what happened this time", over tea and cakes Daniel and Clara told the couple the story of when the Mouse King first appeared, that he had taken over the castle and cast the spell on Daniel again,

Nick signed "Why did you not tell me he came back? I could have helped you" he said in frustration.

But Daniel shook his head in denial "I was going to but the Christmas Angel said I had to get Clara"

The Snow Queen nodded "And a good thing too because now that Clara and the necklace is with you the tracker should not be able to find you" she said beside her husband.

Just then Captain Snow walked in happily "This is a huge palace, you should see it Miss Clara"

Beside her Daniel frowned and observed Clara "She does not have too because she was living in a palace herself" everyone stared at her, the Captain confused, Daniel suspicion and the couple in gentle silence.

"What happened to your house on the fields Miss Clara?" Captain Snow asked.

Clara shifted in her seat, getting uncomfortable with the staring but before she could speak a little snow fairy with a pink and blue sparkly ballerina dress flew nosily into the room and sat on to the Snow Queens left shoulder "You sent for me my Queen…..oh good evening Prince Nick, Prince Daniel, Captain Snow and to you Princess Clara" the little fairy had a high pitched voice that sounds so close to a mouse.

Everyone stared at her for a minute then Daniel turned to her "Why did she call you a Princess?" he asked in confusion.

It was the Snow Queen who answered "Because Daniel, Clara is a Princess" she nodded to Clara "Go ahead dear, tell them" she comforted her.

Clara signed "It is true, I am a Princess…Princess Clara Marie De La Tour but I just found out after my father died, he was a Prince of a beautiful country then he met my mother and he wanted a normal life for Timmy and I....we were brought to a pink palace where we met our grandparents"

Daniel squeezed her hand and said "I am sorry about your father" Clara smiled up at him even as her cheeks were growing red, Prince Nick and the Snow Queen shared a knowing smile.

Then the Snow Queen cleared her throat so everyone paid attention "This is Trixie, one of my snow fairy dancers, she will help you get into the Mouse Kings palace" she said with a smile.

Trixie bravely nodded her head "Yes my queen" the fairy chuckled with a salute.

The Snow Queen glided to the glass doors that lead to the gardens, she pointed at the darkest path "Follow that path into the forest and it will lead you to the Mouse Kings palace" Captain Snow saluted her while Clara and Daniel said their goodbyes then began walking along the path into the trees with Trixie following.

Prince Nick wrapped his arms around the Snow Queen and smiled as he watched his brother leave "Did you see his face when he looks at Miss Clara, he is in love" the Snow Queen nodded silently, Prince Nick frowned at her saddened face "What is it love?" he asked.

Finally she signed and looked at him "I can feel them, they love each other deeply but they could never be together, not when she lives in one world and he lives in another"

Prince Nick's expression turned dismayed "So there is no hope for them then?" he asked as he wanted his brother happy.

She looked up at him "There is away but they must pass the test first" suddenly the Snow Queen smiled and pulled Prince Nice inside "Come on" she said "let us go see an old friend of mine".

Back in the dark kingdom the Mouse King was in a rage "THAT BLASTED SNOW QUEEN" he picked up a small wooden table and threw it agents the wall leaving behind a large crack that was almost to the ceiling "Get the best guards I have and find them" at his last words the fearful guard ran out of the room and shut the door loudly after him, the Mouse King tried to breathe through his fury as he looked out at his kingdom "Coro" he shouted.

Coro walked into the room wary of what the angered king would do "Yes my lord"

The Mouse King turned around to look at Coro "I want you to do something for me"

Coro nodded for him to continue "What is it you wish, my lord"

The Mouse King put a hand on his shoulder "Go out there, find that woman Clara and bring her to me" Coro raised his eyebrow in question, the Mouse King smirked and said "There are two uses, first she can lead the Nutcracker to me and I want her, she will be my queen" Coro nodded and left the room, the Mouse King sat down into his chair then called "Guards"

The top guard rushed in "Yes my lord" he said with a bow.

"Cancel the search, Coro will deal with it" he instructed. The guard bowed again "Yes my lord" he then left the

King to his thoughts.

Clara and her friends were walking along the path towards the dark palace, Trixie sat on Daniel`s wooden hat "So what do we do now?" Trixie asked Daniel.

He looked up at her "We have to release my guardians from their magic prison" he said to the group.

Captain Snow stopped and stared at him in shock "God, I did not know he had your guardians locked up, I am sorry my friend" he said sadly.

Daniel shrugged "I will get them out....so Clara how you find being a Princess?"

Clara shook her head "I do not know but I heard my grandparents talking about me, they think it is time I was married" Daniel`s head snapped towards her knocking Trixie off, his eyes wide and mouth hanging open then he shook himself from his shock.

Captain Snow made a noise "I think Trixie and I will go on ahead" but Clara nor Daniel paid them much attention, so he strolled on away from the pair.

"They cannot force you......who would you marry?" though Daniel was not Sure he wanted to know.

Clara signed sadly "I do not know but whoever he is….. he would not be you" they starred at each other, everything disappeared then Daniel signed.

"Oh Clara" he gently took her hand and kissed her knuckles careful not to give her splinters "If we could be together, I would have made you my queen years ago but we came from different worlds" Daniel pressed Clara's palm on to his rough cheek and gave her a sad smile "I have loved you since we were children, everyone knew it, even my brother noticed I have changed" Daniel pulled her gently into his hard arms "Tell me my love, even if we have to leave each other later, tell me how you feel" as he spoke Daniel rubbed his face into her hair, closed his eyes and smelled her scent.

Clara put her arms around his neck, it was then that she realized he was not hard or rough, his body and hands were soft and gentle, Clara looked up to see Daniel's human face, no wood anywhere, she placed her hands over each side of his face and looked into his pain filled eyes "I have always loved you Daniel….my nutcracker" pulled his face down towards hers.

But before their lips could touch they heard Trixie's cry's and Captain Snow shouting "Put her down you rascals" Clara and Daniel looked at each other then ran down the path, as they were running Clara turned to see that Daniel was a nutcracker again and began to wonder how he became human before.

They found three men, two in front of Captain Snow keeping him back and the third one was behind them, his big hand had a grip on Trixie, the three men wore black cloaks, their hairs tied back but the one at the back had a huge scar on the side of his face, starting from his forehead, down near his right eye and ends at his chin. Daniel draws his sword and took one step forwards but the leader just laughed and held Trixie upside down "Come and get her, young Prince" Captain Snow drew his own sword and growled.

Daniel and the Captain readied themselves to jump over the two front men when Clara said "Captain Crone" everyone paused, some in confusion while others in shock, they all turned to stare at Clara, she slowly walked to the leader, the two men surprisingly let her past while Daniel was trying to pull her back behind him. The leaders hands began to tremble so Trixie easily pulled herself free, the leaders silver eyes widened and fixated on Clara's face, she smiled and took his hand in which held a hidden knife, she prayed his fingers open letting the knife full from his graph and throwing it aside. Clara held his hand in both of hers and when she looked into his eyes, she could see darkness in them, Clara signed "I wish your spell was broken" her necklace began to glow a yellowy white light which swelled around both of them, then the leader Captain Crone fell to his knees, held his head and screamed, only when the light stopped did he opened his eyes to look at her, now she could see his normal blue eyes without the darkness.

Just after nightfall the group made a fire and brought around giant logs to sit on, Captain Crone sat on one side of Clara while the nutcracker sat on the other, Trixie had positioned herself on Daniels wooden hat and Captain Snow with the two other men Jackson and Bill sat opposite them.

They was eating pieces of bread and cheese when Daniel asked "So Captain Crone.....where have you been all this time, the last time we saw you, you was fighting the Mouse Kings second in command, what happened?"

Captain Crone signed and put down his food before turning to Daniel "Well, after my battle with the Mouse Kings second in command I was badly wounded so I stayed with the Snow Queen and Prince Nick, for a while I rested then went into the forest to find you, my prince but the Mouse King found me first and cast a spell to turn me evil"

Trixie smiled over at Captain Crone "You are not evil anymore, Clara took care of that" she said giggly.

He turned to face Clara "How did you break my spell Clara?" he asked her.

It was Daniel who answered while placing a hand softly on her shoulder "The Christmas Angel gave Clara a necklace, so she had 5 wishes but now we only have two"

Captain Crones eyes broadened "You have seen the Christmas Angel?" he gasped in jealousy and shock since nobody had ever seen the Christmas Angel before.

Daniel nodded sadly "The Mouse King stole her magic necklace that is why he has so much power" he informed the three men as he finished his bread.

This time Captain Snow spoke up "And we need to get into the dark castle"

The Captains eyes each other until Captain Crone started to scowl at him leaving Captain Snow grinning in amusement, Clara watched them with a little frown "You…I remember you" Captain Crone snapped but Captain Snow just smirked.

"I did not know you two met before?" Clara said as she gave the last piece of her cheese to Trixie.

Captain Snow shrugged and chuckled "Oh, we know each other all right" he happily sang.

Daniel leaned forward "How do you know each other?" he asked.

Captain Snow crossed his arms and leaned back lazily but never taking his eyes off of Captain Crones face "Shall I tell them or you, old boy" when he remained silent Captain Snow turned to the others "I am married to his little sister Morgana but he does not like it very much" he chuckled as Captain Crone's face reddened.

Captain Crone snorted "Of Course, I do not like it, you would get Morgana in to a lot of trouble, she caused a lot

of mischief when you two were first together" he growled at his new companion.

Clara giggled at the two Captains as Daniel chuckled "So you are bothers in law, good luck my friend, you are going to need it" just when Captain Crone began to growl at them as well Trixie flew off Daniel`s timber hat into the air and said urgently.

"Wait" they all turned to look at her frightened face. "What is it Trixie?" Daniel asked.

Trixie pointed down the path "I sense the mice, they are coming this way" she said fearfully, Daniel and Captain Snow stood up, each grabbing their swords as they moved.

Daniel turned to Captain Crone and his two men "Are you with us" Daniel asked as he held out another sword for him, they starred at each other until Captain Crone nodded and took his sword "Go down the path, do nothing until I get there" the men nodded and left, leaving Clara alone with Daniel, Trixie sat in the highest tree to watch the mice. Daniel turned to Clara and took her into his arms "Clara, please I want you to stay here where it is safe, I cannot fight if you are in danger"

Clara smiled up at him "Do not worry, I will stay here safe and sound…be careful" then she kissed him on the cheek, Daniel smiled, turned his back and walked away with a torch in his hands. Clara watched as Daniels tall wooden form disappeared into the night, she sigh silently

"I love you" she whispered to herself. Clara started to clean up the camp sight and when she was about to dump another log on the fire she saw Trixie cowering in the trees, whimpering, Clara frowned "Trixie…what are you doing up….." but Clara was cut off by a hand over her mouth.

As soon as Clara started getting drowsy she realized there was a cloth over her nose and mouth, her eyelids slowly closed as the stranger spoke "It is a shame that I do not have time to play with the snow fairy" then everything went blank.

Daniel watched as the five mouse guards run away like cowards, he looked at the overs to see Captain Snow frowning "Is there something wrong with this picture, I mean there was only five of them"

"Yes" Daniel replayed "And the Mouse King would not just send five unless he had something up his sleeves"

Captain Crone nodded "Then there must be something he wants from us, the guards was probably a distraction" the Captain said thoughtfully.

Daniel frowned deep in thought while walking slowly back towards the camp sight, he started walking faster as he realized what the king desperately wanted and understanding touched his eyes, Daniel broke into a run as fast as a piece of wood can as he shouted at the others "You are right Captain Crone, he sent them here to distract us" both the Captains ran on either side of him.

"Why, what is he after?" Captain Crone asked.

But it was Captain Snow who answered "Not what Crone but who, the Mouse King is after Clara" through their exchanged Daniel stayed silent, dreading the truth as they reached the camp site. It was a giant mess. Food was scattered everywhere, clothes was torn to shreds, the fire was dyeing down and Clara was gone.

"Jackson" Captain Crone ordered "Put some wood on the fire and not the nutcracker" he said when they took a step towards Daniel before turning to the other man "Bill, see if there are any tracks" they nodded and took off, leaving the others to look for Trixie.

Daniel dropped to his knees, his head in his hands "I have failed her" the Captains looked down at their distraught friend and prince then at each other for they have never seen the prince so defeated in his life.

Captain Snow kneeled beside him and placed a hand on his shoulder "Don't give up now my friend, we will get her back" he implored.

But Daniel shook his head at Captain Snows words "No it is no use, I have lost her, even if we do defeat the Mouse King again, we live in different worlds…..we can never be together" Captain Snow and Captain Crone dragged him near the blazing fire and sat him silently on the logs.

Minutes later Bill returned to site beside Jackson after whispering the news in Captain Crone's ear "The tracks leads to the mouse kings palace so whoever it was they have taken Clara to the Mouse King" Captain Crone said and placed a hand on Daniel's other shoulder "We cannot give up, if we do Clara will have a far worst fate with the Mouse King….maybe there is a way for you to be together"

Again Daniel shook his head "There is no way around it" he said in despair.

Suddenly the fire changed in to a light blue and a voice called out from it "There is a way" Daniel looked up to see the Christmas Angels image in the fire smiling gently at him "Daniel, there is a way to have a future with your Clara" she said as the other men stared in shock.

"How?" he asked.

She shook her head at his question "That is for you to find out" just as she appeared the Christmas Angel vanished into the fire, Daniel gave a big smile "We will be together, even if it takes another 21 years, let us get rid of the Mouse King" the men nodded and cheered as Daniel stood up he started to hear a noise like high pitched screaming "Everyone stop and listen" he said suddenly.

They all remained quiet until a tiny voice shouted out "Hello…is anyone there, get me out of here"

Captain Snow frowned "Is that Trixie?" he asked the others in confusion since they thought Trixie was taken too.

Daniel called out "Trixie, where are you?" "Prince Daniel, I am in here"

"Keep talking Trixie, I will find you" Daniel followed the sound to a can that was dumped on the ground near the forest, he gently picked it up and placed it on a level service.

Captain Snow scowled "They put her in a can?" he growled in anger.

Jackson shrugged then smirked "Well she is no bigger than a bug"

"HEY" they smiled when they heard Trixie's annoyed voice then Captain Crone took out a knife that was hidden inside his boot.

As he reached for the can Daniel grasped his wrist and asked "What are you doing?"

Captain Crone raised his eyebrows "I am going to use the tip of the knife to open the lid, it is safer then us using our hands" Daniel nodded and released him but watched him closely, Captain Crone slide the tip of the knife in to a dent of the lid then with a little twist of his hand the top sprang open and out flew a very angry Trixie.

"Look what that rotten mouse did to my dress" everyone laughed at the little fairy's fury "When I get my hands on that Coro I will"

"Wait" Captain Crone demanded "It was a mouse called Coro? Are you sure"

Daniel glanced at his face to see him turn pale "What is it Captain Crone?" he asked a bit worried the man might have a stroke.

Captain Crones hands turned into fists, his face now turning red "It was Coro I met in the last battle but I thought he was dead unless….Trixie, did you get a good look of him?" he had to ask.

Trixie stared at him then nodded "Yes, why?"

"Think back, did this mouse have a full tail" the men looked at him in confusion but he ignored them, all his attention was on the fairy, when Trixie shook her head he signed "It is not Coro but his son Coro JR, when I killed his father years ago he attacked me but he missed, so I cut his tail in half as a warning and let him go"

Daniel frowned "Why did you let him go?" he asked as the first war with the Mouse King all mice that attacked was arrested or killed.

Captain Crown signed "Because he was only 13 years old at that time"

Daniel nodded understanding his reasons then he turned to Trixie "Now Trixie can you tell us what happened when we left" Trixie floated over to sit on Captain Snows shoulder

"Well, I was playing in the trees with the baby birds when I was Coro coming up behind Clara, I was really scared then he grabbed her and placed a cloth over her face" Trixie sniffed as tears fell down her face "Then Clara fell asleep and Coro carried her off but not before he stuffed me into that smelly can"

Daniel nodded "Ok this is what we will do, we will sneak into the palace, get Clara and free my Guardians from their prison" he glanced at each person "Is everyone ready" Daniel waited until they nodded then began running towards the dark palace, in there he knew the final battle would begin.

In the dark palace, in one of the many bedrooms Clara began to wake from her deep sleep, slowly she opened her eyes to found that she was in a large black coloured room, she pushed herself in a sitting position, there was a large dresser with designs on it, a big window with bars attached to it on the inside and she was lying in a huge round bed with colorful covers. Clara looked down to find herself wearing a long white dress, a slit down the skirt to revile one leg, her bodice tight and pushing her breast up and her shoulders and neck was bare, on her feet she had on white high heels shoes. Clara carefully got up and walked to the door, she grabbed hold of the doorknob and started twisting it but it wouldn't turn, Clara signed as she walked back to the bed and sat down, Clara was trying to find an escape when she heard footsteps coming towards her door then a key turning the lock, the door burst open to reveal the Mouse King himself smiling smugly at her, the Mouse King was dressed in a white coat also his breaches were black as were his boots, his arms were crossed in front of him but Clara could see the crystal shaped necklace around his throat, "So" Clara said "Why have you brought me here?" she demanded.

But the Mouse Kings grin only grew bigger "Because my dear, you are about to become my Queen" Clara starred at him afraid of his meaning.

"What are you talking about?" Clara asked fearfully.

The Mouse King stepped into the room causing Clara to stiffen "It is quite simple Clara, you and I marry by sundown"

At his words Clara shook her head, standing up she glared at him "I will never marry you" but the Mouse King smirked, never taking his red eyes from her beautiful face.

"I believe…you have no choice" the Mouse King held up his hand and click his fingers, at the sound two guards strolled into the room and each grabbed a hold of Clara's arm then started dragging her out the room.

The Mouse King walked ahead down the halls while Clara tried to break free from the guards and as they entered another room Clara cried out one name "Daniel".

• • •

Down below in the dirty dark dungeons Daniel pushed himself out of a hidden hole that he had to crawl through, he helped pull up the others then went to a deserted table, Captain Snow walked to his side "Where is everyone… there should be lots of guards here?" Daniel asked him but Captain Snow just shook his head silently.

"Here" Jackson called pointing to a cell that had a front make of glass, Daniel walked over to stand by the man and there in the cells, sitting on the ground were his guardians. They wore old silver with a bit of gold armor over their chests, black breaches and long sleeve t-shirt, they hairs was long and dirty while their faces were grey with dark circles under their eyes.

Daniel drew his sword and took a swipe at the glass wall but the glass didn't even have a crack. At the new sound instead of the quiet cell they looked up at Daniel and as soon as they saw him they crawled to the glass "My prince, can you hear me?" one of the men asked.

Daniel nodded "Yes Martin, Jason what is happening to you?" he asked warily.

Martin the guardian with bigger shoulders and black hair shook his head weekly "We don't have much time Daniel, you have to get the necklace from the Mouse King, if you don't break this spell then we will die….this prison is sucking our life's and magic from us" he moaned in pain.

Jason with red hair nodded "But you have to get it now, he will be distracted by his wedding"

Daniel paused then frowned "What wedding?" Martin signed and shifted "To a woman named Clara, it is happening now" Daniel and the men stared at them in shock.

Then he looked angrily at the others "let us go stop him once and for all" everyone nodded and ran towards the stairs.

●●●

In the secret door that was hidden behind the kings chair Daniel could see a scared looking priest with a book in his hands, his voice vibrating around the room, the Mouse King on one side was smiling brightly and on the other was Clara in a beautiful white dress but she was struggling agents two guards who had hold of her arms, he also saw his people now human and out of the prisons, raged coursed through him, for what the Mouse King has done and was trying to do so while the priest was speaking

Daniel stepped out of the door and into the throne room shouting "Stop" everyone gasped, at the sight of not only seeing their prince alive but turned into a nutcracker again.

Clara stopped and stared at him with love in her eyes, it was the love he saw that gave him strength "Daniel" she whispered.

The Mouse King pointed at him while shouting "Get him" but when the guards began to rush towards their beloved Prince the people finally reacted by attacking the mice so the whole throne room was filled with fighting. Clara gasped as the mouse guards kill innocent people, she looked around in horror as the priest fainted and the Mouse King leaped towards Daniel with his sword held high, on the over side of the hall Captain Snow and Captain Crone were attacking Coro together.

Clara heard a cry in the air, she looked over to see Trixie pointing in Daniel's direction "look Princess Clara, the Mouse King has Prince Daniel backed agents the wall" Clara glance over to see that Trixie was right, Daniel was agents the wall as he and the Mouse King took swipes at each other, Clara turned to Trixie and whispered into her little ear, Trixie flew across the room as fast as she could and before he knew what was going on, Trixie ripped the necklace from the Mouse Kings neck. Daniel pushed the Mouse King away from them just as Clara saw more mouse guards coming at him and she remembered that she had two wishes left.

"I wish the mice had no weapons" the heart glowed a light blue color this time and as she watched every weapon that the mice had disappeared.

Knowing he had nothing left the Mouse King ran towards the doors yelling "Retreat" every mouse ran but before he can reach the doors, men in dark blue uniforms strolled in and surrounded the mice, Daniel looked at the door to see the Snow Queen, Nick and the Christmas Angel enter.

Nick nodded to the men "Put them in the dungeons" the men lead the Mouse King and his mice to the deepest, darkest part of the dungeons, as the people cheered Daniel took Clara, the Captains, Nick, the Snow Queen and Christmas Angel into the dungeons where Martin and Jason was being held.

Clara gasped at the state of them but the others were not surprised, the Christmas Angel tapped the glass then shook her head "I cannot help break this spell because the Mouse King had it for so long, it will take time to fix my crystal" she looked sadly to Daniel "I am afraid this is out of my hands"

The Snow Queen observed the glass then turned to Clara "There is away but it will be your choice Clara. You can use your last wish to free the guardians or you can be with Daniel for the rest of your life"

As everyone turned towards her Clara said "What about Daniel's spell"

The Christmas Angel hit herself with her hand and shook her head "I forgot, sorry Daniel, I have some magic left to change you back" she waved her hand over Daniel's form then his body began to shimmer and a glowing mist surrounded him, a minute later the mist slowly disappeared. The first to appear was a pair of black boots, then white breaches with long strong legs, a tight long coat of red and white colors with broad shoulders and finally his face, his mouth thin and long, his eyes which was always a lovely blue was now was filled with strength and wisdom and his black hair pulled back from his face. Clara smiled but had tears in her eyes as Daniel walked towards her and took her into his now soft but strong arms, from the corner of her eye Clara saw the others turn away to give them privacy, Daniel signed as he gave her small kisses over Clara's face.

"God Clara, I feared I would never hold you in a warm embrace or kiss your lovely face…..I love you, my Clara I love you very much" he said as he held her close.

Clara backed away while shaking her head "Oh Daniel, I do love you, more than anything but we cannot, we got only one wish left and your guardians are dying" Daniel's expression shattered, pain replacing joy, his pain clear in his eyes but he nodded.

"Your right" he said in defeat, they each saw their hearts breaking at the thought that they could never see each other again. Clara stepped near the glass as the others joined them.

Nick looked over at his brother to see a broken man, there was great pain in his eyes that Nick wished he didn't have to see, Nick shared a knowing look with his wife, Clara touched the necklace "I wish all the Mouse Kings spells was broken" the heart glowed red and spread over the glass and around the room, when the glowing light stopped the glass was gone, the guardians was standing strong on their own feet and clean again.

They walked over to Clara and each kissed her cheek "Thank you" they said.

Clara managed a small smile until the Snow Queen stepped forward "Clara, it is time to go" Clara nodded and said goodbye to everyone when she turned to Daniel, he held out his arms so Clara hugged him tight to her. Clara felt something wet touch her face and looked up to see tears down his cheek, she gave him the last comfort she could by pushing herself up to press her lips to his in a his, the Snow Queen put a hand on Clara's shoulder and suddenly her body began to fade.

Before she was completely gone Clara looked into Daniels eyes just as her own tears fell and said "I love you Daniel" then she was gone.

Clara opened her eyes to see light coming through her bedroom windows, she was wearing her nightdress and her hair in a platt "Daniel" Clara whispered as a single tear fell down her face.

Just then her door burst open and Timmy rushed in too jumped on the bed "Clara its Christmas, it's finally

Christmas….what is wrong Clara?" Timmy asked as he saw the tears in his sister's eyes.

She shook her head and smiled into his concerned face "Nothing come on, let us see what presents Santa have brought us"

"Oh right" Timmy shouted, after her breakfast Clara and Timmy left to play outside.

They would open their presents that evening, "Merry Christmas my loves" Elle did not know what was wrong with her daughter but there was something broken about her, she turned to her in-laws "Did you noticed the way Clara was today" she asked her in-laws worriedly.

They nodded "Yes" the Queen said "I believe she is in love but with who?" they were just talking about it when one of the butlers came in.

"Excuse me my lord but there is a young man here who wish to speak to you and the Queen" the man said.

The King nodded "Show him to the library George" he said as he and his wife stood up from the table.

The butler nodded then bowed "Yes my king".

— • • • —

Clara was building a snow man with Timmy, she wore a long red coat and her hair was hanging around her back while Timmy wore a blue coat, black breaches and a green hat, then the butler George came over and said "Princess Clara, the King asks for you to come to the library"

Clara stared at him as Timmy whispered "Oh boy you are in trouble"

George cleared his throat "This way please" Clara followed him through the doors, down the hall and into a large room filled with books on several shelves, ladders and a desk with three chairs, behind the desk was the King with the Queen standing by his side and a young man with his back to her sitting in one of the chairs.

The King stood up, took his wife's hand and walked to the door "Clara" the king said "There is someone here to meet you…we will be outside if you need us" Clara nodded as she watch them leave then signed.

"Hello Clara" Clara stiffened, her heart beat faster at the voice, slowly she turned to face the man who was now standing there watching her with loving blue eyes.

Clara gasped while tears came to her eyes, the she ran towards him and threw herself into his arms saying one word "Daniel" their arms held each other.

Clara crying happy tears as Daniel kept kissing her then said in a sweet voice "Oh my darling, I have come for you" he buried his face into her hair as he breathed her scent.

Clara pushed back to look into his face "but how, we were in different worlds"

Daniel smiled "When you was given that choice, the choice to save my Guardians or stay with me, it was a test and you have chosen the right one, the Snow Queen and Christmas Angel cast a spell to send my kingdom into your world so we can be together"

Clara frowned "Wait…..when the Christmas Angel said the necklace was damaged she was lying?" she asked in shock as she thought that the Christmas Angel would never lie.

Daniel laughed at Clara's thunderstruck face then kissed the look away "Yes, so now we can be together my love but I got one question" Daniel took hold of Clara's hands and went down on one knee "Clara Marie De La Tour, will you become my wife"

Clara smiled, fresh tears coming to her eyes "Yes Daniel Luke Bowe, I would love to be your wife" Daniel slipped a red heart diamond on to her finger and they kissed for the brightness of their future.

9 years later

Daniel walked into his bedroom to see his lovely wife leaning over the crib watching their 1 month old son sleeping. He walked over and wrapped his arms around her "Happy anniversary Clara" he said happily as they watched the sleeping baby.

She smiled at him over her shoulder "Happy anniversary Daniel….how is our daughter sleeping?" she asked as she knew that their three year old Kathrine was a terror before bedtime while her twin brother John was always good.

Clara chuckled when Daniel huffed "It is always hard getting Katharine asleep, John is better for going to bed" Clara nodded and smiled, Daniel turned Clara around "I have something for you my darling" out of his pocket Daniel handed her a present.

"A book?" she said after opening it "The Nutcracker….. oh our story" she exclaimed with happiness and excitement.

Daniel smiled "Well close to it, I love you, My Clara" he said in a soft voice.

Clara throw her arms around him "As I love you Daniel……finally my own nutcracker returns" from that day on their story was spread throughout the world to every child and down each generation, they began believing in Clara and her nutcracker. Daniel and Clara then lived happily with their children and grandchildren in their happy ending.

THE END